Bogey Roads

and other polluted poems

Paul Hymas

Copyright © 2020 Paul Hymas

All rights reserved

ISBN: 979-86-48995-22-2

To Claire

I'll find my way home

Acknowledgements

I'd like to thank many people who have helped along the way, but in particular;

Steve C whose illustrations are simply fantastic.

Annie Barnard and her husband Chris Walker. Chris's amazing music accompanies most of the videos on my YouTube channel. Annie has patiently proofread everything I have thrown her way. She has the patience of a saint and is a wonderful lady. The world needs more people like Chris and Annie. Granddaughter, Serena, also deserves a thank you.

A big shout to Gibson Talbert, who has given me superb technical advice for my channel. He has also given me incredible emotional support during a real tough time for me personally. I will always be grateful that he took the time to show me what caring really is. My thanks, said here, is the very least I can do for such a man of honour and integrity.

Thanks also to Esther who came up with some wonderful ideas and encouragement.

To a very special friend in America who, I hope, will be in a much better place one day.

To Kat Wakefield, a superb journalist, a lovely person and an all-round good egg.

To my family and friends who have supported me as I got to where I am now.

And finally, to Claire. If it wasn't for her then none of this would have ever happened.

CONTENTS

Page

1 - 2	Bogey Roads
3 - 4	Dreamland
5 - 6	Bake me a Cake
7 - 8	Farting Game
9 - 10	Isobel
11 - 12	Lost Socks
13 - 14	Aunt Smelly Breath
15 - 16	Family
17 - 18	Knock-Knock Poo
19 - 20	Green Fingers
21 - 22	My Windy Bottom
23	Nits
24 - 26	Mum- do not bend
27 - 28	Earwax
29 - 30	Witches Secret
31 - 32	Genius of Fluff
33 - 34	Dine-oh

Bogey Roads

I'd been saving bogies for quite some time,

when an idea struck to help with crime

And if the police agreed with me,

they could have my bogies all for free

So I wrote to them with my plans,

to slow the cars, the bikes and vans

Instead of tar, where they drove too quick,

they could lay my bogies **REALLY** thick

No more cameras 'round the town,

use my bogies to slow them down

'Cos even trucks with heavy loads,

cannot speed on bogey roads

And added with the note I'd shipped,

a jar of bogies freshly whipped.

The police wrote back, yes, they were keen,

but did not want the roads turned green

And PC Logan did some tests, (with the hope of more arrests)

with a model car that did a bunk, but car and driver simply sunk

So if a car was full-size weight, fleeing crooks could suffocate

And one more thing, the inspector claimed,

there might be problems when it rained

He hoped my ego had not been bruised,

a great idea, just can't be used

But there's one thing that I could do,

was send some more, he was short of glue.

Dreamland

Dreamland is a funny place, you dream some crazy things

Last night when I was dreaming, I saw a cow with wings

Flying like a jumbo jet, across the sky she sped

Then started dropping cow pats that landed on my head!!

I sheltered in a garden hut, away from soaring cow

Then froze in panicked horror, cos I heard a tiger growl

I tiptoed 'round the corner, concerned I'd be a snack

But tiger was a giant horse with a jockey on his back!

I climbed out through the window and on the roof I sat

I came face to face with Morris, a talking pussy cat

He whispered to be careful of hyenas telling lies

And of the fluffy bunnies, who were meerkats in disguise

I left him talking to himself and ran along a path

Saw pink and yellow parrots, swimming in a bath

Saw a bunch of monkeys barking, at penguins in a tree

And piggies building houses, I'm <u>sure</u> that there were three

A giant panda slithered by, acting like a snake

He turned and started singing, 'It is time for you to wake!'

I didn't want to listen, the dream was crystal clear

But then my dog was with me, drooling in my ear!

Bake me a Cake

The yukkiest cake that I have had

Was made for me by my Dad

He used some milk and mouldy cheese

And rotten eggs if you please

A tea bag taken from the bin

Some apple cores and banana skin

Squashed tomatoes, cold baked beans

All sorts of veg, including greens

Half a fly and half a spider

And toenails cut from Auntie Ida

He went outside to get some coal

Then squeezed a spot into the bowl

He baked it slow, he sliced it thick

I ate a piece and then got sick.

Draw your own illustration for Bake me a Cake

Farting Game

Who wants to play a farting game, boys or girls it's just the same
Just grab some things that give you wind, like olives stuffed or haggis tinned
All sorts of drinks to loudly slurp, to help you puff and bottom burp

So several friends of mine and me,
sat beneath the garden tree
All gathered round to win the prize,
for grunting long and big in size
Extra points for eggy smell,
and farting loudly does quite well

Hoping that it went to plan, we parp and toot best we can
We guff and trump, we cut the cheese, 'cos judge and jury we must please
We hiss, we farp, we let 'em rip, we finger pull for showmanship.

One-gun salutes are such a laugh, I like them most when in the bath
'Cos they're the ones that are to be, the only farts that you can see
A few more honks and rattlers too, then time is called and we are through

So later on, we've took a pause, huddled up to count the scores
Lew's the champ with all the flair, he's been the best at bending air
He's won it with a work of art...his two-toned, triple, blaster fart.

Isobel

My tooth fell out but just my luck, the fairy had to come by truck
By truck, you ask, why was that? Because her wings are just too flat
I was woken by the engine's noise, and the fairy's lack of graceful poise
Then as she bent to reach my fang, the elastic in her dress went 'twang'.

She sat there crying and began to squawk,

so I thought it best that I should talk

I asked her name and asked her why,

she came by truck and did not fly

'I'm Isobel', she said through tears,

'And I haven't flown for several years

'You see', she gasped, 'I was bad,

'so wings got clipped, I'm really sad.'

I held her in my hand and sighed, and waited 'til her eyes had dried

Whatever had she done so wrong, to stop her flying for this long

She said that all that she had done, was laugh out loud and poke some fun

When her boss, whose name was Joe, kicked the curb and stubbed his toe

Punishment was then bestowed, she'd have no choice but go by road

And to further hurt the poor old thing, he removed, from her, all her bling

So when you next have fairy's call, and notice tyre tacks real small

Jump up screaming, shout and yell,

'My tooth's been got by Isobel!'

Lost Socks

How do socks just disappear?
It happens several times a year
Is there a place with evil King,
who sells the socks his gofers bring?
So I got online and Googled out,
to all my mates I gave a shout
I searched around to find some news,
about losing things that go in shoes
No search results did I achieve,
'bout missing socks and why they leave
I sat confused, scratched my head,
and questioned why my sock had fled
To try and find where it had gone,
would mean a sock-search marathon
I searched the house from top to toe,
where on earth do these socks go?
As time approached for search to scrap,
a message dropped to favourite App.

T'was from a pal with ear to ground,

he had the facts on story found

When socks get lost without a trace,

he said he'd found there was a place

The place itself is up near Leicester,

and run by girls whose name are Esther

It was time to form a partnership,

me and Dad, a research trip

Up to the place where socks are took,

to find this beastly master crook

Screaming like a senseless clown,

to living room I hopped on down

I grabbed the door and burst right through,

and told my Dad all I knew

Dad briefly hit the button; mute,

reached to a pocket in his suit

He gave me cash for clothing store,

'If you need socks, just buy some more!'

Aunt Smelly Breath

The wife of my Great-uncle Geoff, has really awful smelly breath
The strangest mouth you'll ever see, a furry tongue & teeth, just three
So a visit always goes like this, she wants a hug and sloppy kiss
She'll grab and hold her face to mine, sending shivers down my spine

Mum and Dad insist I'm wrong, no such thing, no smell or pong
But they don't have to get to grips, with Aunty Edna's aging lips
So last time that her dreadful reek, had left me feeling rather weak
I thought it best to have a chat, to uncle Geoff about just that

He told me in a whispered voice, that he was left with little choice
He has to stuff his nose up full, with loads and loads of cotton wool.

Draw your own illustration for Aunt Smelly Breath

Family

I have an uncle, uncle Fred. Big in size, bald of head

His many talents make me laugh, like singing opera in the bath

And without working up a sweat, he can fart the alphabet

Great Gran Mabel is something weird, with funny ears and wispy beard
And despite her ugly, saggy bits, she can grow stupendous zits
These get burst with skill that's rare, and thick green puss lands everywhere

Then there's Leia who is so cool, she's super fun and beautiful
My favourite aunt without a doubt, who juggles marbles with her snout
And given speakers with echo mic, can loudly burp a song you like

My brother Russ is on this list, due to fate with added twist

But don't be sad and shed your tears, he really loves his hairy ears

Plucked twice a day and weaved with twigs, and sold to men as chinny wigs

Billy Kite, it has been proved, is a cousin twice removed

You may believe that it's not true, his unique snot is coloured blue

And bubbles blown from bulbous nose, are shown-off proud at county shows

I understand that we don't choose, our family and who's are whose

And despite my own being strange, given choice, I would not change

'Cos even Dad, who's dull and duller, can poop, I'm told, in technicolour

Knock-Knock Poo

I'm not that sure to tell you, but really this is true
All about a friend of mine who did a Knock-Knock poo
I know that you're confused right now and you will have some doubt
But once I've told you all I know, you'll have it all worked out

Some time ago when he was sat, Rob heard a little plop
He thought that he should take his time, there might be more to drop
And then he heard a little voice, his poo he heard had spoke
And as my young friend listened in, it told a knock-knock joke

This really got him snorting, with laughter he did roar
And as he sat there grinning, a voice said there were more
'Go right ahead' Rob urged him, and gave his poo a clap
Could there be any better, than knock-knock jokes on tap?

But this 'aint the good news story, that you were wishing for

'Cos Robert was forgetful and did not lock the door

In burst his older brother, a trickster and a cheat

And went to flush the toilet, with Rob still on the seat

He really was so helpless as he loudly tried to plead

But his brother was successful and carried out the deed

A gurgled voice did splutter as it disappeared from view

But washed out to the sewer, was poor old Knock-Knock poo

Green Fingers

Whilst sat down one night, after scoffing a pear,
someone I know did something quite rare
He stuck out a finger and cut his own nail,
and put it away to let it go stale
Much later on, some six weeks or more,
he went to the desk and opened the drawer
He took out the box with the nail inside,
and went to the garden, filled up with pride

He had a nice pot, that he'd covered in foil,
and filled it right up with slightly dry soil
He dropped in the nail and covered with dirt,
watered it gently with a small little squirt
To the end of the garden and placed in the shed,
then locked up the door and went up to bed
He checked the next morn and thought it was wrong,
'cos already the stem was some four inches long.

It just kept on growing, quite impressive in size,

Its strange little leaves were attracting the flies

Parts of the plant had buds to be seen,

these tiny small things, a weird colour green

Another month passed and despite everything,

the buds kept on growing, like pieces of string

And as they got longer, they'd sway in the breeze,

and for a peculiar reason, they attracted the bees

It was late in the summer, can't remember the day,

when an expert came calling to take it away

Then followed a text, from an egghead called Rose,

before the nail was cut, had he picked at his nose?

Cos she'd looked at the data and what it had shown,

was a bogie with roots, hence a snot plant had grown

She also informed him it was now in the bin,

she was fed up of getting, green gunk on her skin.

My Windy Bottom

I trouser coughed the other day,

and scared my poor old dog away

It smelt so bad, it wasn't nice,

and to make it worse, I did it twice

I took a sniff, it made me sneeze,

it smelt of eggs and rotten cheese

Can you believe that such a thing,

could make the budgie fall from swing?

Then Dad walked in, now that was funny,

his eyes went red and his nose all runny

He stared at Me, was I to blame?

'No', I said, 'The outside drain.'

He stood there sniffing with a frown,

(whilst I wondered if my pants were brown)

Then my bottom burped once more,

'It wasn't you?....are you sure?'

Draw your own illustration for My Windy Bottom

Nits

Something on my head is twitching
    Feels so weird, my hair is itching
        I guess it means that they are back
            The dreaded nits, the bugs in black
                Every night I'll wash my hair
                    Drown the things, I don't care
                        I listen close and hear them say
                            That won't work, we're here to stay.'

                            I find it strange that things so small,
                        Will use my skull to have a ball
                  Playing Simon Says within my thatch,
              They'll run around and make me scratch
            I bet they sing and dance as well
        Annoying me and raising hell
    All these things to make me cringe
From back of neck to wonky fringe

Out it comes, the metal comb
    Rid those creatures from my dome
        Followed by, on Doc's advice
            Special cream to kill the lice
                No more fun and games for them
                    Hair all rid from tip to stem
                        Scalp all clean, none to kill
                            But they'll be back...I know they will.

Mum – do not bend

Mum liked the thought of yoga,

but had trouble from the start

The first time she did 'downward dog',

out popped a tiny fart

She'd been watching vids on YouTube,

'bout how good it makes you feel

Their promise she'd be fitter,

was, I think, the main appeal

She ordered spongy knee pads,

a thick, long yoga mat

A lycra top and leggings,

and a load of this and that

She started with some basics,

and turned to me and grinned

But as I've said already,

she had trouble with the wind.

She carried on regardless,
the dog just left the room
She tried position 'Scorpion',
which really made her groan
I watched my poor old Mother,
a hand I could not lend
Even when she had to do,
an angled forward bend

A 'Dolphin' pose then followed,
then 'Eye of Needle' next
It was when she tried the Lotus,
to dad I had to text
My Mother had got stuck there,
Dad raced in from the shed
Untangled both her feet and legs,
and took her up to bed.

He came down minutes later,

laughing as he went

He said that she would try again,

but I knew what he meant

Her Yoga days were over,

she'd leave behind the squats

No more bending backwards,

and getting tied in knots.

Earwax

If you play with it enough,
wax from ears is useful stuff
Keep it warm and soft to touch,
then use it well to do so much

        I, myself, like to mould,
        all sorts of things that you can hold
        I once produced a paperweight,
        a mug for nan, a dinner plate

                But other things can be made,
                for which, I'm sure, you could be paid
                What about a model boat?
                Made with wax, it's sure to float.

Create some art that you could sell,

use on hair instead of gel

And if it's soft and nicely ripe,

it will fix a leaking pipe

        Candles are a useful thing,

        made from wax and bits of string

        There's endless things you can do,

        with careful hand, wax and glue

                So every time you wash your ears,

                for the next, say, twenty years

                Keep all the wax for goodness sake,

                you never know what you could make.

Witches Secret

Now don't be fooled that witches broth,
has eye of newt or nose of sloth
No tooth of wolf, no wings of bat,
they're not mixed in, don't think that
You think you know, (or may have heard)
but there is no Tawny Frogmouth bird
And witches really do think twice,
before adding frogs or tiny mice

No flaky skin off zombies' clothes,
no bogies picked from Parson's nose
No Brussel sprouts or gingerbread,
no dandruff from a hippy's head
No warts hacked off from turtle's neck,
no blackheads in, they double-check
And do they gather round at night?
That's another myth that isn't right.

So let me be the one that tells,

what witches use to make their spells

But if I'm caught, I'll tell you now,

they'll use a spell called 'Change to cow'

So quick, before the witches show,

these are the things you need to know

It's hard to guess but it's really true,

they use....moo moo moo moo moo moo moo

Genius of Fluff

A friend of mine, old Harry Hutton, gets lots of fluff in belly button
He collects it from the time he wakes,
and you'll be amazed at what he makes

He's made several ties, to wear with suits and big long laces for his boots
A tablecloth and patchwork quilt,
a sporran and a tartan kilt

His wig is made from all the bits that he didn't use for winter mitts
His cowboy hat, his shorts and Crocs,
made just the same as knee length socks

The gloves he made and slippers too, are dyed a lovely shade of blue
The pillows made that don his bed,
are sort of coloured, pinky red

I've often asked how it's done, is it weaved or is it spun
But he just smiles and with a sigh,
says, 'It's really easy if you try.'

I don't know how he does it though, I can't get fluff to have a go
I check my tummy every day,
there's not enough, there's just no way.

Draw your own illustration for Genius of Fluff

Dine-oh

I have got the weirdest pet and Dine-oh is his name
He fell and really hurt himself and wasn't quite the same
He got a nasty cut, you see, and from this the blood did pour
So then I had a pet at home, who was a Dine-oh sore

A day or more then passed us by and I noticed that his claws
Had begun to grow much longer, as they poked out from his paws
He then refused to munch upon, the meat I served at lunch
He only wanted vegetables and bananas by the bunch

He seemed to stop his barking, his skin went kinda' pale
And it looked like there were feathers, growing on his tail
His hair was that much thicker, he started to gain weight
The vet had no idea at all, he could only speculate.

I took him out for walkies, as you're supposed to do
He ran around excited, then dropped a number two
This was rather smelly, it was huge and it was green
It really was the biggest poo that I had ever seen

Once I got him home from walk, I bathed his poorly cut
I was pleased that it was healing, so he got a coconut
That night he slept quite peaceful, more restful if you like
His breathing like a scooter, and not a motorbike

The weekend was upon us and round came uncle John
He had asked to see the feathers but, on looking, they were gone
His claws were also smaller and he didn't look so fat
And he'd left his bowl of veggies, for Fred the ginger cat

In a week his fur was softer, his nose again was wet
He ate a pound of chicken, the best that I could get
His poo was back to normal, I couldn't ask for more
I love that he's a dog again, and not a Dine-oh sore.

Printed in Great Britain
by Amazon

LAURA Y FRANCESCO